# RESCUING THE BRIDE

## MAIL ORDER BRIDES OF NEBRASKA

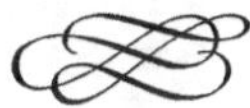

### SUSANNAH CALLOWAY

Tica House
Publishing

Sweet Romance that Delights and Enchants!

# PERSONAL WORD FROM THE AUTHOR

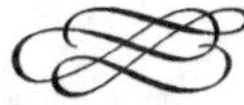

**Dearest Readers,**

Thank you so much for choosing one of my books. I am proud to be a part of the team of writers at Tica House Publishing who work joyfully to bring you stories of hope, faith, courage, and love. Your kind words and loving readership are deeply appreciated.

I would like to personally invite you to sign up for updates and to become part of our **Exclusive Reader Club**—it's completely Free to join! We'd love to welcome you!

**Much love,**

**Susannah Calloway**

**VISIT HERE to Join our Reader's Club and to Receive Tica House Updates!**

https://wesrom.subscribemenow.com/

# CONTENTS

# CHAPTER 1

From among wisps of feathery clouds, the sun threw great spears of light across the sky, the final blows of a dying warrior. The golden rays painted everything in colors so brilliant they made Hotah's eyes hurt—the somber green of the plains that were rolled wide open all around him, the navy of the sunset sky that extended over him, and the simple mound of earth that swelled from among the deep grass at his feet. It would be difficult to notice that bump in the dirt if one wasn't looking for it. Hotah could hardly believe that this was all that was left of something that had been his entire world.

His knees ached. Standing still was nothing new to him; he'd spent hours blending in with trees and rocks, waiting for a deer to come past within range of his bow. But the sunset reminded him that he'd been up here on this hill for hours. It was time to go back down, and yet Hotah couldn't bring himself to leave.

How had it been a year already? He passed a hand over his face, pushing back strands of hair the color of obsidian. Sometimes it felt like she'd been gone for a lifetime. There were other times – infinitely more painful – between sleeping and waking that he would roll over on his grass bed and reach for her, and she wouldn't be there.

"*Atè! Atè!*"

The piping voice reached Hotah a few moments after the quiet footfalls he'd tried to ignore. He lowered his hand from his face, letting the warm breeze dry his tears, and turned. His sorrow melted in the eyes of the baby who was being carried toward him. The child leaned against her grandmother's arms, chubby hands extended to him, a giggle bouncing from her throat. "*Atè!*" she cried again.

"*O opa la.*" Hotah held out his hands, allowing the little girl to scramble into his arms. She giggled, throwing her arms around his neck. Hotah smiled over her shoulder to the older woman who had carried the baby to him. "Thank you, Mama. I would have been back soon."

Mama nodded, but there was something questioning in her eyes, which were the warm black of coals before burning. "Winona was asking for you," she said. "As you can see."

Hotah allowed himself to cuddle the little body of his

daughter close for a few moments. She smelled a little like her mother always had; he buried his face in her tumultuous black hair. Mama took a step closer, rested her hand on his arm. "I'm sorry, *ciksi*. I know today must have been very hard for you."

Hotah tried to smile. "It wasn't easy," he admitted. "I… I miss her so much, Mama."

"I know. So do I. So does everyone," said Mama. "Your wife was a wonderful person. Once in a lifetime." She squeezed Hotah's arm. "It has been difficult for all of us since she walked on. But she is safe now, Hotah. You know that."

"I know," he said. "I just wish she was still here."

"We all do," said Mama. She laughed then, tickling little Winona's chubby tummy. "Except perhaps this one – she's far too busy to worry about such things."

"Oh, is she?" Hotah couldn't stop himself from chuckling. He turned Winona over onto her back, cradling her in one arm as he brushed the tip of her finger against her cheek. It had the same golden undertone that her mother's used to have, bright and warm as the last rays of the sun that was sinking rapidly behind him. "And what are you being so busy with, *o opa la*?" he asked the baby.

She squealed. "*Atè!*" she said again, grabbing for his finger with her fat little fists.

"She's trying her best to make her grandmother old, that's

what," said Mama, laughing. "Crawling everywhere as fast as a running deer. She'll be walking before long."

"Walking." Hotah felt a swift pang of pain. "I wish Mina could see it," he murmured.

"Mina," said Winona. She stared up at Hotah with her lustrous dark eyes. "Mina!"

"Yes, Winona," said Hotah. He raised the baby to his face, breathing her scent, and kissed her smooth forehead. "Mina was your mama, and she loved you like I love you – forever."

Winona fell silent, gazing at him. Hotah felt as if his heart would break. He wished Mina could be here for moments like these as their daughter began to pick up new words.

"Come on, Hotah," said Mama quietly. "It's time to go back down to the village."

"I suppose it is," said Hotah softly.

It took all of his strength not to look back as he followed his mother back down the hill, the sacred high place where his wife's bones lay.

# CHAPTER 2

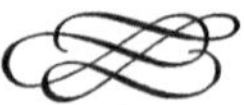

Lina Sterling slid a cheap tin tray out of the oven, careful not to let the few roast potatoes slide off it. They were small and pitiful enough already without being squashed, too. She put them down on the stove and let go of her apron, wiping her burned hand on her threadbare dress.

"There, Mama," she said. "Potatoes are done."

"Good," said Mama from the other side of the kitchen, where she was stirring a pot of something that even smelled watery. "How many are there?"

Lina smiled apologetically. "Six," she said. "Sorry, Mama. There was one for each of us, but one of them was green."

Her words seemed to bow Mama's shoulders a little further, as if adding to the giant burden that was bending her mother's stick-thin frame in half. Once, Mama had been lovely, Lina thought. She remembered a time when Mama's pleasant round cheeks had been rose-bright, her green eyes dazzling. Now, she was as faded as the dress that slumped hopelessly around her thin figure.

"It's all right," Mama said, turning back to the pot. "This is ready, too. Call your siblings and father."

There was no need. As if magically summoned by the smell of the baking potatoes, four children spilled through the kitchen door, each somewhere on the scale between "ragamuffin" and "urchin". Their clothes were all out-at-the-elbows and oft-mended, and even though they bounced around with limitless energy, Lina could see that all four little faces were growing paler by the day. They clamored around Mama as Papa dragged his frame through the door and slumped down at the kitchen table, which wobbled dangerously.

Lina pressed her hip against the table to stop it from toppling over thanks to its one rickety leg. "Calm down, everyone." She laughed. "Come on. Sit down and we can give you some dinner."

The word *dinner* proved to have a magical effect. The four siblings arrayed themselves instantly on the wooden stools around the table, their wide eyes following the tray of potatoes as Lina brought them to the table. There was Joe, who was twelve; Maggie, nine; Peter, seven; and Amy, four.

Lina divided the biggest potato in half for the two little ones. She felt a pang in her heart as Mama followed with the stew pot, dropping a spoonful of watery vegetable stew on each tin plate beside the potatoes.

Papa still smiled up at her as if she'd just bestowed a feast of meat and cake upon him. "Thank you, my dearest," he said, grabbing one of Mama's hands and raising it to his lips.

A hint of color returned to her cheeks. "Oh, George," she said. "Don't be such a flirt." But she was pleased.

Lina took her place between Maggie and Joe and held out her hands to them. They placed their cold little fingers in her palms, and she clutched them tightly, bowing her head as Papa said grace. His voice rolled around the room, the only rich thing in their lives. "For what we are about to receive, may the Lord make us truly thankful. Amen."

"Amen," chorused the children.

Hungry though she was, Lina paused for a moment to watch as the four little ones tucked in. Mama was smiling at Papa with a happy, secret expression that made Papa blush and quickly look down at his meager dinner. Lina bit her lip to hold back her amusement.

Papa cleared his throat a couple of times. "Maggie, Joe," he said. "How was school today?"

"Oh, awful," said Joe, with his mouth full. "Old Rabbit-mouth made us do so many sums, I thought I'd die."

"Joe!" said Mama. "Don't talk with your mouth full – and *don't* call your teacher names."

"You haven't seen him, Mama," said Joe, swallowing and mopping at his mouth with the back of his sleeve. "He's got big yellow teeth and these funny black whiskers just like a rabbit. I wouldn't be surprised if he lived in a smelly cold hole in the ground, too. He's that much of a wet blanket."

"It's still not nice," said Mama, clearly struggling to hide her amusement.

"I hope you had a better day, Mags?" said Papa.

"Oh yes," said Maggie. "My day was lovely. Thank you, Papa."

The sweet girl beamed at him, and Lina felt as though her heart was being squeezed. This family deserved so much better than a tiny apartment on the top floor of a drafty Boston building.

"Did you have any luck looking for work today, Lina?" asked Papa.

Lina sighed. "I'm sorry," she said. "I've found nothing."

"She's been helping me with the sewing," Mama chipped in. "I've gotten much more done this week than I thought I would – it'll be a little extra."

"Not as good as a job," said Lina. She watched as Joe stared down at his empty plate, clearly still hungry. Discreetly, she pushed her half-finished potato across to him.

"Lina, it's not your fault that you haven't been able to find anything," said Papa. He gave her a warm, genuine smile. "Boston isn't an easy place to live in. We all know that."

"Everyone's suffering with the job cuts," said Mama. "Your papa was lucky to have kept his position at the factory."

Lina didn't want to think about what would have happened if Papa hadn't kept his job.

"We still have a roof over our heads and food on the table," Papa added. "Don't worry, my darling. You'll find something."

Lina tried her best to smile, even though it was a struggle to believe his words. "Thanks, Papa," she said. "I hope so."

She did hope so, because she knew that they couldn't keep this up much longer, not with the children growing by the day. Winter would come, and there would be no fuel for the fire. Worry clenched tight in Lina's gut.

She had to do something, or her family could starve.

Winter's edge had long since left the cool wind that found its way through Lina's holey scarf and onto her soft skin, but it was still chilly. Sometimes she felt as though winter never truly left Boston despite the fact that the month of June was slipping rapidly between her fingers. It seemed to linger in the stern stone of the buildings that pressed around her, hiding in the shadowed alleys, secreted deep in the eyes of the men on the street when they raked Lina with chilling glances.

She clutched her basket a little closer to her chest, feeling how light it was on her arm. Even the bits of sewing that Mama was able to do seemed to be growing fewer. At least taking the baskets of clothes back and forth between the handful of clients and the house made her feel a little more useful; Mama's arthritic knees weren't up to it anymore.

It was a relief to step out of the narrow little back alleys and into one of the town squares lined with shops. There were fewer strange, wild-eyed street men here; instead, young women seemed to be everywhere, walking together in knots with shopping baskets on their arms. Lina tried not to be envious of their elaborate dresses and pretty little hats. She did slow for a moment, though, lingering in the lovely square as she gazed through the shop windows. Oh, if only she could buy a whole dozen of those beautiful white rolls in the bakery window! She could just imagine little Amy's eyes lighting up at the sight of them, the sighs of contentment as her hungry family tore into the delicious food. Lina's heart felt so empty. She knew her family couldn't keep this up for much longer. But what was there to do to save them?

A knot of women clustered around one of the newly-finished buildings on the corner of the square caught Lina's eye. Curious, she turned her path toward them. The women were all young, she noticed, and they giggled and jostled one another as they kept a few yards back from the front door. Something was definitely going on.

Lina spotted Mabel, one of the girls she'd grown up with, in the crowd. Hoisting the basket a little higher on her arm, she greeted her. "Good morning, Mabel. How are you?"

Mabel turned, a smile lifting her rich, walnut brown cheeks. "It's nice to see you, Lina. We're all well. And you?"

"Fine, fine," said Lina breezily, trying not to let her eyes dwell too long on the patched and faded state of Mabel's dress. "What's going on here?"

"Oh, don't you know?" Mabel giggled. "It's a new Mail Order Bride agency! It's just opened, in fact. I think these girls are all trying to pluck up the courage to go inside – I'm just curious."

"Mail Order Bride agency?" said Lina. "What's that?"

"Well, apparently the West has too many men, and the East has too many women," said Mabel. "There's a lot of girls down here looking for a new life in the West – and a lot of men who've made a life for themselves there, and they're ready for a bride, except there aren't any girls out there for them to marry. So they ask an agency like this one to find them a girl who'll go out West."

"Out West?" Lina felt a ripple of excitement. "It must be

wonderful out there. Why, I don't think I've ever been more than ten blocks from home."

"I don't know. It sounds awful frightening to me," said Mabel. "Think of all the wild animals and savages out there."

"I don't think any people are really savage," said Lina. "Just different, that's all."

"I guess you're probably right." Mabel shrugged. "Anyway, I've no reason to do such a thing. I'm marrying my Carl soon – and we may be poor, but we're happy."

Lina sighed. "So is my family," she said, "but I don't know how much longer we can do this – not with the children growing every day."

Mabel rested a hand on her shoulder. "I'm sorry, Lina. I can't imagine what it must be like, trying to feed all seven of you, with your papa earning a pittance at that factory."

"It isn't easy. But maybe it would be easier if one of us wasn't home," said Lina, her brain moving fast. "There's gold out West, isn't there? The men there must have money."

"Oh, Lina!" Mabel stepped back, her eyes widening. "You can't mean… you can't be thinking about signing up, can you?"

"I can and I will," said Lina firmly, her mind made up. "And my way would be paid. Even if all I achieve is to get out of the house, it'll already help my family."

"Surely, you need to speak to your papa first."

"I will," said Lina. "If there's a man out there that would want to marry me, of course. But there's nothing stopping me from signing up."

Mabel shook her head. "Think about this, Lina. What would it be like to leave the city and travel thousands of miles away just to marry someone you've never even met? It would be terrifying."

Lina thought of Joe, polishing off his supper at a gulp, left hungry afterward night after night.

"It would be worth it," she said.

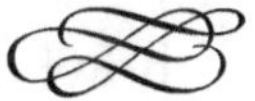

# CHAPTER 3

A fortnight came and went, and Lina didn't hear a word from the Mail Order Bride agency, even though the sweet older woman behind the counter had promised to let her know by mail if there was any match to be found for her.

Her heart weighed in her chest, heavy as an iron shackle, as she packed the freshly mended clothes into her basket on a mid-June morning that was much too cheerful for her dark mood.

Mama held out a stocking for her, neatly darned. "Are you sure you don't want something to eat?" she said.

"No thanks, Mama. I'm all right," said Lina, flashing Mama a smile despite the fact that hunger was ripping at her belly with savage claws.

"You had nothing for supper last night, though."

"Oh, it's all right. I wasn't hungry," said Lina.

Mama was watching her with hooded eyes. Lina could tell that she didn't believe her, but she didn't want to tell Mama the truth: that she'd seen the disappointment in Joe's eyes when she set down another bowl of insipid gruel in front of him. The boy never complained, but she knew how hungry he was. Lina leaned forward and kissed Mama on the cheek.

"I'll be back soon," she said.

"Thank you, darling." Mama rested a hand on Lina's cheek, her eyes filled with love and pain.

"And I'll stop by the agency and check with them about a match," Lina added.

"Oh, Lina." Mama sighed. "I know your papa told you that it was all right, but I'm not so sure about it."

"We don't have a choice," said Lina gently. "It's the only way, Mama. There's no work here for me, and the children are hungry."

"I suppose you're right. It's just… such a long way away." Mama shook her head. "I love you."

"I love you too, Mama."

Lina was deep in thought as she moved through the streets, her feelings a messy tangle of confusion. She wasn't sure what to hope for today: that she'd find a match at the agency, or that she wouldn't. *No,* she decided as she stepped into the market square and saw the handful of women waiting as ever at the agency's doors. *I do hope I have a match. Nothing could be worse than watching my siblings starve – not even leaving them behind.*

All the same, nervousness knotted in her gut as she joined the queue. She'd hardly come to a halt when the man at the door beckoned to her.

"You!" he said. "I remember you. You're Lina Sterling, the first girl that signed up here."

"Yes?" said Lina, nervous.

"Good. Come on in," said the doorman. "We've got news for you."

There was a murmur of jealousy in the queue. Lina felt her heart flip; she rested a hand on her chest as if to calm it. "Me?" she said.

"Yes, you. Come on," said the doorman, holding the door wide open.

Feeling the pressure of the others' eyes on her, Lina walked into the building. It smelt cloyingly of pink roses and chamomile. The elderly woman behind the desk, kind as ever, was busy jotting something down in a book when Lina came in. She looked up over half-moon spectacles and smiled widely.

"Lina!" she cried. "The brave first girl to sign up." She sat back, removing her spectacles. "I'm pleased that you came by. I was just going to write you a letter."

"Good morning, Mrs. Redford," said Lina, trying not to fidget with nervousness. "Wh-what were you going to write me about?"

"I've got a match for you." Mrs. Redford beamed. "A lovely young gentleman from Planter's Point in Nebraska."

*Nebraska.* Lina didn't know how many thousands of miles away that was, but she'd looked at the map of the United States a few nights ago, and she was sure that it was all the way on the other side of the country. Or of the world, perhaps. She forced a smile. "Is that so?"

"Yes, it is." The woman chuckled with excitement. "His name is Corbin Wedge, and he sounds lovely. A real rugged cowboy type, you know? Just the kind of exciting man that an adventurous lady like you is looking for."

Lina had to admit that he sounded fascinating. "What does he do?" she asked.

"He's a businessman. Very successful, by the sound of it," said Mrs. Redford. "He owns plenty of land."

"It sounds nice, Mrs. Redford," said Lina. "I'll let you know this evening – I just need to speak to my parents."

Mrs. Redford paused. "Lina," she said gently. "I don't want to put you under pressure but look at all those girls outside. They're looking for exactly the same thing that you are." She spread her hands. "If you don't say yes now, I promise you, someone else will before the hour is out."

Lina closed her eyes. There was nothing else for it, and a thrill of excitement filled her. She was heading out West to marry Corbin Wedge, a mountain man, a cowboy of the big sky country. A grin spread across her features.

"Well, then, let me say it now," she said. "Yes, I'll go."

"Good." Mrs. Redford beamed. "Stop by a little later this afternoon, and I'll have everything ready for you."

Lina walked out of the building, feeling as though her feet were barely touching the ground. She could hardly believe how quickly her life had changed.

# CHAPTER 4

Winona rose slowly, her fat little legs bowing under her weight. The baby's face was creased in an expression of fierce concentration as she held both of her chubby arms out straight. For a moment, she waddled forward, and Wichapi thought her granddaughter was about to pitch forward onto her face.

Hotah crouched a little nearer from his seat on a log near the baby. He held out his hands, his face transfixed with a grin that Wichapi hadn't seen in months. "Come on, *o opa la*," he murmured to the child. "You can do it."

Hotah's voice seemed to give Winona extra strength. She drew herself up, hands reaching out to her father, and took a wobbling step forward. The little foot patted quietly on the sand, then another as she stumbled forward. Her steps grew increasingly wobbly until she collapsed – straight into Hotah's hands. He scooped the giggling baby into his arms and kissed her forehead.

"Beautiful!" he said, beaming at the child. "You can walk!"

Winona squealed in delight, kicking her legs. Hotah laughed and lowered her to the ground. "All right, then," he said. "Off you go." He patted the child on the head as she flopped to her hands and knees and crawled off busily.

"That was wonderful, *ciksi*," said Wichapi. She came over to Hotah and lowered herself slowly onto the log beside him, feeling the pangs of her aging bones. Hotah held out a hand to help her down. "Thank you," Wichapi said.

"It was wonderful, wasn't it?" Hotah sighed, joy and agony mingling in his eyes. "She looks just like her mama, especially when she's concentrating."

"She'll grow up just as beautiful as Mina was," said Wichapi gently.

"I wish Mina could have been here." Hotah looked away. "She only held the child for a minute before the pain of that labor took her."

"Mina walked on to a better place," said Wichapi. She wrapped an arm around Hotah's shoulders. "But I know that you miss her. All of us miss her."

"All of us but Winona," said Hotah sadly. "She doesn't even know that she's missing an *ina*."

"No, but that doesn't mean that she doesn't need one," said Wichapi.

Hotah glanced at her. His hooded eyes had turned black, like the sky before a storm comes. "What's that supposed to mean?" he asked sharply.

"Don't be angry with me, Hotah," Wichapi chided.

"I'm sorry." Hotah sighed.

"I love you, *ciksi*. And I love your little one. I just want what's best for both of you."

"I know."

"And I'm just beginning to wonder…" Wichapi hesitated, trying to read her son's dark eyes. "Hotah," she said. "You know that Winona can't grow up without a mother."

"I know," Hotah repeated. He still refused to look Wichapi in the eyes.

She rubbed his back, the way she used to do when he was a little boy with a skinned knee. "Don't you think that it's time to start thinking about taking another wife?" she said gently.

Hotah stood up. His voice was low, but there was something broken in his face. "I'm going hunting," he said, stepping back toward his tipi.

"Hotah…"

He was already walking away, disappearing beneath the buffalo hide flap of his home. She could hear the rattle of wood as he gathered his hunting things. Letting out a sigh, Wichapi got up and scooped little Winona into her arms.

"We won't be seeing your *ate* for a few days, little one," she murmured. "I just wish somehow that he will find peace for his restless spirit over Mina's death."

Winona giggled, uncomprehending, and tugged at Wichapi's long black braid.

"For your sake as well as his," Wichapi added.

The huffing of the engine and the gentle roll of the train had been nauseating two days ago when Lina had first boarded the steam train. It had settled a bit now, for which she was grateful. She'd hardly ever seen a train in real life before; she'd been excited to ride in it, even though tearing herself away from her family had been like ripping off one of her own limbs. Now, that pain of parting had become a duller and more persistent ache, and the excitement of the train ride had long since worn off. Lina just wanted to get to Planter's Point.

She leaned her head back against her seat, grateful for the luxury in which her new fiancé – Corbin – had chosen to bring her to his home. She'd never eaten so well in all her life. Still, she was starting to tire of the constant motion of the train, and the landscape that had changed so rapidly in the beginning of their journey had been mostly the same for miles and miles. The whole world seemed to have been reduced to a great, flat, blazing green plain that stretched in all directions. Lina was starting to realize why this place was called "flat water land".

They were in Nebraska now, at least, and it was only a day's travel before she'd reach her new home. Excitement ran through Lina's body. She couldn't wait to tell her family all about her new life.

For now, though, she had to get through a few more hours of boredom. Picking up her fading copy of *Arabian Nights*, she began to read. The slow beauty of the words and the rhythmic mutter of the train tugged at her tired brain, and in a matter of minutes, Lina's eyelids drooped close and she sank into a peaceful darkness.

Her doze was torn apart by an appalling sound. Sitting bolt upright, Lina gasped, her book tumbling to the floor. The sound was a deafening squeal – a long, ripping noise, the scream of agony that twisting metal would give if it had a voice. Beyond the ear-splitting sound, Lina could hear hoofbeats, and a wild yipping. For a moment, she remembered Mabel's words about savages. Was she about to be scalped?

"What's happening?" she gasped to the passenger sitting across from her.

The young woman clutched at her little boy, drawing the child onto her lap. Her eyes were wide and white-rimmed with fear. She shook her head mutely.

Lina slid across her seat to the window, peering through the blinds. For a moment, she saw nothing; just dust devils twirling across a green plain. Then, a horse and rider charged into her vision, and a gasp tore itself from her lips. Silver flashed on the horse's saddle and bridle; its rider wore a black bandanna tied around his face, his hat pulled low over glittering eyes, and a pistol shone in his right hand. There was another on his hip.

Lina pulled back.

"What is it?" cried the mother.

"I…" Lina began.

There was a deafening crash. The door of the compartment was kicked open, and a figure towered over them, his shadow falling long and black over Lina and the mother and child. He had a tremendous shock of bright-blond hair, glowing pale gold around his head; the eyes were wide and dancing with life, and when he grinned, his teeth were crooked and capped with gold. A pistol smoked in his hand. "Howdy, folks," he crowed. "You've got yourselves a hold-up.

Down on the ground and don't make a single noise, you hear? Get down!"

Lina's heart was pounding in her ears. She scrambled to her hands and knees, throwing herself to the floor of the train; the mother and child were whimpering in fear somewhere nearby. The man stomped closer to them, poking through their bags.

"There's nothing in there that's worth stealing," said Lina.

"Shut up!" the man barked.

The little boy let out a thin whine of terror. "Hush, hush," his mother whispered. "Please, darling. Be quiet."

Lina could hear the frightened murmurings of the other passengers. Heavy footsteps moved back and forth among them, harsh voices resounding all over the train. She hugged the floor, feeling panic pounding in her gut, struggling to quell it. This was a little more adventure than she'd bargained for.

The little boy let out another whimper of fear, and the blond man stomped to a halt beside the mother. "Quit that noise!" he barked. "Silence the child, girl, or I'll put a bullet in you both."

The mother's voice was hysterical. "Please, love, please, be quiet, be quiet," she cried. "Please. You need to be quiet now."

Her frightened tone did little to reassure the boy. He started to cry louder, and the man took a threatening step nearer. "I'm warning you, girl," he growled.

Lina lifted her face from the floor to watch as the terrified mother clutched her child, tears pouring down her white cheeks. "I'm sorry, sir," she panted. "I'm…"

The man dealt her a swift kick in the belly with the tip of his boot. The woman cried out but didn't release her grip on the child. "Shut up!" he barked again.

Lina had had enough. She sat up. "Leave them alone!"

Her voice rang around the compartment. The blond man froze, and so did Lina's blood. He turned, his face wearing a dangerous sneer. "What did you just say?"

"Leave them alone," said Lina again. She folded her arms. "They're just scared. Take whatever it is you want and go away. Leave them."

The man took a step nearer to her. The sneer twisted into an ugly scowl. "Let me tell you something, little Eastern missy," he purred. He reached out, and his fat fingers seized her chin, forcing her to look at him; they smelt of cheap tobacco. "I'm Max Blackmore, and no one talks to me like that. I rule these plains."

Lina felt her resolve melting. She trembled, but she couldn't back down. "You don't rule me," she said.

The blow came out of nowhere. The back of his hand rang

across her face with breathtaking force, and she fell to her hands and knees, gasping in fear and pain.

"I rule everything," Blackmore spat. He grabbed her arm, yanking her to her feet with a force that wrenched something in her shoulder. "You're coming with me."

"No!" Lina cried, trying to pull away from him, but it was like trying to pull out of a grip carved from solid stone. She found herself being dragged down the aisle by the brutal robber – heading for an uncertain fate.

# CHAPTER 5

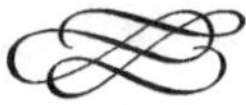

Hotah placed his moccasins carefully. The buffalo hide had been worn soft by the years; it made no more sound on the grass than the shadows of the clouds chasing one another hither and thither across the plain. He was moving up a hill now, and the terrain was growing rockier as he reached the outcropping at the top, but he'd seen the group of white-tailed deer grazing among those rocks. His grip tightened on the bow in his hand. It was a graceful thing, carved of a single piece of green ash, and the horsehair string that held it was trembling with tension. It hummed as though it could already taste blood.

The wind stirred his long, dark hair, running its cool fingers against his scalp. He relished it, feeling the world dissolve into this single moment, past and future falling away in favor of sharp focus on the present. Hunting was a time when it was no use to remember.

He'd nearly reached the top of the outcropping now, and he could hear the gentle rip of grazing deer. Staying downwind, he began to circle around, and when he passed by a boulder at the very top of the outcropping, he saw them: a cluster of fine young deer, their coats shining hazel in the sun. His quarry was off to one side. It was an older doe, her flanks still fat, but the flesh of one hind limb had been torn in ribbons by some hunter's claws. Hotah would finish the job – and the doe would feed his tribe.

There was a distant sound, a rhythmic puffing, and Hotah glanced over his shoulder. The railroad was a stitched scar across the face of his beloved plains; on the horizon, a white cloud of stream heralded the arrival of a gleaming metal monster. A steam train. Hotah's heart hammered. He had only seconds to take down that doe before the train was upon him. Plucking out an arrow, he laid it on the string, his fingers folding around the wild turkey feathers that fletched it. The ash creaked as he drew the bow, aiming the arrow high – high enough to float through the distance between them and punch into the heart of that old, injured doe.

His fingers were trembling on the string when the crack rang out. The sound seemed to set the deer on fire. They leaped into the air, their tails flicking up to show the bright white undersides. Slender legs drove them forward in floating leaps; they disappeared among the boulders, emerging beyond them on the plain, their fleet forms vanishing toward the horizon.

Hotah lowered his bow. He'd barely had enough time to feel frustrated before there was another deafening bang, much closer this time, and he realized that the sound was more than just some mechanical clank of the oncoming train. It was a gunshot.

Hotah bolted. Fleeting as the deer, he raced back behind the nearest boulder and threw himself into its shadow, panting. The train was close now, its thunder growing; he could hear the rhythmic hammer of hooves on the earth. But they weren't coming toward him. After a moment, he heard a long, appalling squeal; the shriek of metal on metal. Slowly, he peered around the edge of the boulder, an arrow still on the string.

The train was slowing down. Sparks flew from its wheels, the steam from its chimney decreasing. On either side, there were horsemen galloping alongside. Their jaded horses were lining out for all they were worth; silver flashed on their saddles and bridles, the sunlight glinting off revolvers in the riders' hands. Another shot was fired into the air; Hotah heard its whistle, saw the smoke puffing from the revolver. The men all wore hats pulled down low, their faces muffled by black cloth, and he saw spurs slamming into the flanks of the horses as they strove to keep up with the train.

He was watching a train robbery.

Hotah froze, lowering his bow. It would be no good against an entire posse of outlaws.

The horses were jogging now, the train slowing more and more until it finally came to a complete halt. Leaping off their horses, the men disappeared into the train.

Hotah was pinned where he was behind the boulder. He had nowhere to run, and nothing he could do. He could only hope that none of them realized he was there.

The barrel of the revolver was a small, cold circle jutting into Lina's waist as the robber dragged her between compartments of wide-eyed people. Breathless from struggling, Lina couldn't find it in her to fight him. When she glanced down, she saw that the man's thick, gloved finger was resting on the trigger; it would take only the tiniest movement, the tiniest jump, to send death ripping through her intestines. She could hardly breathe.

All around her, she could hear whimpers of terror, the harsh rumbles of outlaws' voices among the people on the train. She didn't know what she would do if she heard a gunshot.

Blackmore paused by one of the compartments and rapped on the door. "Boss," he growled. "We've got ourselves a little problem."

The door swung open, and another man stepped out. This

one was small and wiry, yet the way he gripped the shotgun in his hands made Lina fear he was the most dangerous of the bunch. Her fear was confirmed when she looked into his eyes. They were the palest green, and they were filled with death.

"Pretty little problem, ain't she?" he growled, grinning to reveal yellowed teeth and a wad of chewing tobacco pressed up against his cheek. He let go of the shotgun's barrel to reach for her with reeking fingers, and Lina pulled her head back.

Blackmore dug the revolver deeper into her waist. "Watch out, little missy," he snarled in her ear. Old alcohol whiffed on his breath. "You're making the boss angry. You don't want to make the boss angry, do you, then?"

"No," growled the wiry man. His fingers found her face this time, gripping her cheek tightly between thumb and forefinger until it stung fiercely. Pulling her face around, her forced her to meet his eyes. "What did she do?"

"She's a little fighter," said Blackmore.

"Well, we'll have to see about that," said the boss.

"What shall I do with her, boss? Put a bullet in her?" Blackmore's casual tone made a shudder slide down Lina's back.

The boss studied her for a moment, taking his time. His eyes worked their way from her face, down her collarbones, lingering for a long time on her slender waist. She could feel his gaze crawling on her skin, and it filled her with a horror and hatred that couldn't hope to be equaled by the fear she felt of the pistol in her side. After a moment, the boss shook his head.

"She'll still be… useful," he said. "Tie her up, gag her, and put her in the back. We'll soon see about this fighting spirit of hers."

Blackmore gave a dark chuckle. "Sounds good to me, boss." He yanked at Lina's arm, making another burst of pain pop through her shoulder. "Come on."

The pain in her shoulder forced her to move with him, and her heart was hammering in her throat as Blackmore dragged her past the rest of the passenger compartments. They were reaching the cargo cars now and he was tugging her past barrels and boxes and bags where no one would find her if he gagged her and tied her there, and when she risked a glance up at his hungry eyes, she had no doubt about what he would do next. The fear rose in her like bile, burning in her throat.

Sunlight warmed the side of her face. She glanced to her left and found herself staring into open air. The door of the train was open there – she saw a sweaty horse grazing just beyond; they must have come in here – and it offered her a heart-lifting view of the endless plain and the tremendous sky.

"Come on!" growled Blackmore, yanking at her as she slowed, and Lina's mind was made up. There were things more terrifying than the gun at her waist, and she still had one free hand. She spun, grabbing at the gun; Blackmore cursed as her fingers closed around the cold metal cylinder of the barrel, and she felt the weapon jump, heard the crack. The bullet whistled into the wooden side of the train, punching a hole.

Hooves thundered outside; Blackmore was yelling, ripping at the gun, letting go of her arm. She'd wrestled enough times with Joe to know what to do next. Spinning, giving up the revolver as he gripped it in both hands, she rammed her elbow as hard as she could into his face.

There was a crunch when her elbow met his nose. Blackmore shrieked, and Lina saw her chance. She bolted, praying he'd be blinded by the pain, and rushed for the wide-open door. Freedom beckoned on the other side, the cool wind calling to her. She had just enough time to see the drop away from the tracks, the slope beyond, the rocks below. It was still better than staying here with Blackmore. He lunged at her, his fingertips clawing at the back of her dress, and Lina jumped.

She didn't jump down. She jumped out – as far as she could, trying to get away from Blackmore. The world dropped away below her with sickening speed, and for an instant the wind curled around her as if it would scoop her up and sweep her away into the great blue sky. But it didn't. It just screamed in her ears as she tumbled, and the ground was rushing to meet her.

The last thing she heard was the shriek of the train's brakes as they were released, and the engine puffed to life again. Then there was impact, pain, a salt taste in her mouth, a tumbling, and darkness.

# CHAPTER 6

Hotah seemed to spend a very long time crouched behind the boulder, waiting for the sounds of the train robbery to recede. It was one of the hardest things he had ever had to do. As he listened to the raised voices of the outlaws and the screams of the terrified passengers, he had to force himself to stay safely behind the boulder. Every part of him wanted to help somehow. But it would be no use, he knew. What could one man do against an entire posse? All he'd achieve was to get himself instantly killed. There was a certain type of white man that wouldn't think twice about doing such a thing, and he knew that the men robbing the train were exactly that type. He couldn't afford not to get home to Winona.

Still, there were a few moments when he grew perilously close to coming out of his hiding spot and putting a slender, deadly arrow in the chest of one of those robbers. The most perilous of all was when the crack of a shotgun rang out, an insult to the peace of the surrounding wilderness. Hotah had tensed then, but he thought better of it, reminding himself that he had daughter to get home to.

Finally, he heard the sound of the train coughing its way back to life. He waited until the last of the hoofbeats had faded into the plains, and even the white cloud of the train's steam had vanished over the horizon, before stepping out of his hiding place.

There was no sign of the outlaws or the train. Silence had fallen once more, except for the high, haunting cry of an eagle whose wing shadow Hotah could just make out when he squinted up at the evening sun. Except for the railroad, shining softly in the golden light, it was as if white men had never come to this wild land.

Hotah let out a slow sigh as he started down the hill toward the tracks, hoping to follow them back to the copse of ash trees where he'd left his horse. He knew there were people among his own tribe – although not in his own village, thanks to his father – who would say that it would have been better if the white men really had never come here. They had brought so much death to this land, or at least, their ancestors had.

But *Até* had seen the world differently. He'd seen past the color of the pioneers' skin, seeing people instead of races, and Hotah's childhood had been filled with watching his father forge relationships with the whites. Perhaps that was the reason why their village had always been left well alone.

Hotah himself had carried on the tradition of trading with the town of Planter's Point until a year ago. Mina had always loved going to town, seeing the women, admiring their satiny dresses. She'd been friends with many of them, but after she was gone, it was just too painful for him to ride into town.

Hotah shook his head, trying to shake loose the memories that crowded around him, snapping at the corners of his mind like hungry coyotes. He reminded himself sharply that he was on a hunting trip. The train robbery had cost him time that he didn't have. He needed to track down another quarry quickly – before nightfall if he could. His tribe could use the food, and Hotah needed the distraction.

The train tracks were hot to his feet when he stepped across them on his moccasins. They glinted in the sun, bright and unnatural, and Hotah wondered where they'd found so much metal. To find enough metal to connect the world to the Plains must have been difficult. His moccasins were soundless on the gravel as he stepped over the second track and paused at the edge of the steep, rocky slope, his eyes scanning the horizon. Another deer would be perfect right now, but he'd take a squirrel too, if only to feed them for the evening. He could start again in the morning if need be.

He scanned the surrounding rocks, motionless. After the racket of the train, small animals might start coming out of hiding again. His gaze rested on every boulder, waiting for something – a flash of movement, the outline of a furry body, a splash of brightest yellow…

*What?* Hotah blinked, staring closer. There *was* something yellow lying there in the grass, and the shade was unnatural, far brighter than the fawn of the surrounding stones. Hotah squinted. It looked almost rumpled – like a piece of disregarded cloth thrown aside, only much too big.

He took an arrow from his quiver and laid it on the string, keeping a steady grip on his bow as he started to move closer in a half circle, keeping all his senses open. Wherever outlaws went, there was bound to be trouble. He didn't trust this strangely shining object. Moving soundlessly on the rocks, Hotah climbed to the top of a larger boulder and looked down at the yellow thing.

Shock stung his hands and feet. It wasn't a thing at all; it was a woman wearing a yellow dress, lying sprawled on her side, her skirts tossed carelessly over her legs like she'd tumbled to where she lay now. She was very still, and blood oozed down the size of her head.

Hotah thrust the bow and arrow back into his quiver and broke into a run. His breath rushed in his throat as he scrambled from rock to rock, his feet as sure on the rocky terrain as on the floor of his own tipi. In moments he was by the woman's side, crouching down at her head. Her face was gray, her cheeks pinched with hunger beneath the growing mask of blood spreading over her face, and a pang of regret ran through him. It looked like he was already too late. Gently, he touched his fingertips to her wrist. For a moment, there was nothing, and sorrow spread through Hotah's heart. Then he felt it: the barest flutter of a thready pulse, weak and arrhythmic against his fingertips.

Hotah squinted up at the horizon. The woman should be allowed to heal with her own people, yet Planter's Point was too far away. The woman needed help – and soon. Wichapi was her best chance at survival. As gently as he could, he slipped his arms underneath her body, gathering her up against his chest. She smelled strangely floral, and her head lolled against his shoulder, leaving a smear of blood on his bare chest.

He shifted her a little, trying to make sure she was as secure and comfortable as possible, before turning his footsteps back up the tracks to the grove where he'd left his horse. He could only hope that he'd get back to the village in time.

# CHAPTER 7

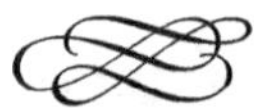

Pain. A constant, pounding pain, like a dull red glow at the edge of consciousness, hammering again and again into the right temple with relentless violence. She wanted to make it stop, but she couldn't move, didn't know what she'd do to stop it even if she could.

She heard a groan and realized it was her own. The sound seemed to drag her out of the darkness, and she tried to open her eyes. For a moment, the pounding agony wouldn't let her, but she fought it down. Sunlight pierced her eyes, and she blinked against it, the pain intensifying as if the beams of light were shards of glass. It ebbed slowly, and she realized she was panting with pain as she stared up at the ceiling – or what should have been the ceiling. Instead, she was looking at a series of wooden poles, lashed together above her head. Some thick, tawny material had been spread over them. She was in some kind of a conical tent.

Lina blinked a few times, utterly confused. What had happened? She needed to look around. She lifted herself onto her elbows, but a stab of pain racked her, the world spinning.

"Shhh." The voice was low and mellow beside her; a knobby hand grasped the back of her neck, easing her gently back down onto the soft, rustling surface she was lying on. "Rest now, little one."

Lina held her breath until the pain faded a little. Her vision began to clear, and she was looking up into a face. It was an aged face, wizened as willow bark, and about the same shade; framed by two long, black braids that were streaked with steel gray. *An Indian!* Yet somehow, she couldn't find it in herself to be afraid. The black eyes that twinkled down at her were much too kind to be frightening.

"You need to rest," said the Indian woman, her voice slow and measured. "You have been hurt."

"Where am I?" Lina croaked.

"Safely in my tipi," said the old woman. "I am Wichapi. You are safe now."

Her English was good; Lina could have listened to her rich accent all day. It leached the fear out of her. "How did I get here?"

"My son found you by the train tracks."

*Train tracks.* The memories flashed back to her: Blackmore and his revolver, the look in his eyes, the fear stabbing into her. Leaping desperately. The crack as she hit the ground. Lina sucked in a breath of fear, and Wichapi laid a hand on her shoulder. "Your head pains you," she said.

"A little," Lina admitted. "How far am I from Planter's Point?"

"A day's ride."

Lina swallowed, feeling tears prickle at her eyes. "I came all the way from Boston," she whispered. "I'm meant to marry a man in Planter's Point. I have to get here. He'll be worried about me."

Wichapi cocked her head to one side, sending one long braid tumbling down over her shoulder. "Do you know him?"

Lina couldn't shake her head, but the look in her eyes must have told the full story. Wichapi nodded slowly. "It's all right. What is your name, young one?"

"Lina."

Something misty came into Wichapi's eyes, and a sad smile crossed her face. "A good name," she said quietly. "For now, you're not well enough to travel, Lina. You need to just stay here and rest."

Before Lina could answer, there was a rustle from

somewhere near her feet. She managed to lift her head just enough to see the front flap of the tipi being pushed aside. A tiny little girl – she still looked wobbly on her feet – stumbled through the flap. She had jet-black hair and enormous, sparkling eyes almost the same color; when she saw Lina looking at her, she froze, staring.

Wichapi chuckled. "My granddaughter, Winona," she said. "She's never seen a white person before."

The child was so beautiful that Lina could hardly remember her troubles. "Hello, Winona," she murmured.

Winona took a wobbly step nearer. Her luminous eyes captured Lina. Wichapi let out another low cough of laughter. "The little one has just learned to walk. She's getting in all kinds of trouble."

"She's so beautiful," murmured Lina.

Winona flopped forward onto her hands and knees and began to crawl, her fat little hands slapping the clean dirt floor. She reached the hem of Lina's dress and tugged at it in her small fingers. Lina reached toward her, holding out a hand to the baby. After a moment's hesitation, Winona touched her skin. She seemed to like its softness and warmth, letting out a little coo of delight. She crawled right up into Lina's arm where she lay and curled herself in a ball, her silky black hair pillowed in the crook of her elbow.

"Look at that!" Wichapi smiled. "She likes you."

"I like her," said Lina. She wanted to stroke the baby's soft hair, but her body ached too much, so she just enjoyed the warm little bundle curled against her waist. She had missed little Amy's cuddles more than she'd thought.

"Winona!" a deep voice called outside. "Winona!"

"Hotah!" Wichapi called back. "She's in here. Come in. Your guest is awake."

The front of the tipi parted again, and a tall figure stooped to enter it. When he straightened, the atmosphere seemed to freeze in respect of his commanding presence. His body was tall and slender, with long, powerful limbs; great muscles stood etched in the burnished bronze of his calves and chest. There was no hair on his face, but a cascade of straight black mane tumbled over his shoulders, richly elegant. His face was as rugged as the boulders of the plains he called home, and his eyes blazed with the intensity of burning goals. Something about them made goosebumps rise all over Lina's skin.

"This is my son, Hotah," Wichapi said, her voice filled with pride. "He's the one who found you."

Lina realized she was gaping. She cleared her throat, but her voice still came out as a discombobulated squeak. "Thank you for saving me," she managed.

Hotah gave a single nod. His eyes dwelt on the contented baby for a moment, and Lina thought she saw the flicker of a smile crossing his face. Then he said, "I was just looking for Winona," in a voice that rolled with the depth of lakes, before turning around and disappearing from the tipi.

# CHAPTER 8

Lina couldn't take her eyes off the willowy figures of the Lakota. The firelight flickered on skin that gleamed polish bronze, muscles rippling as the men moved as one, their bare feet landing in perfect time to the drums that raced like her heart all around the fire. She realized she was leaning forward, her hands gripping her knees through her worn yellow dress as the sound of the drums vibrated through her entire body. It was intense now, furious, the men moving together with the speed of an approaching storm, snatching her breath away.

She spotted him in the midst of them: Hotah. His lithe body twisted and leaped, his mane a black torrent over his shoulders, eagle feathers bouncing and lifting with each movement. His eyes burned hotter than the coals of the fire. As the crowd of men spun around the blaze, there was one moment when Hotah was directly opposite her, and for an instant his eyes locked on her own. Her mouth grew very dry, and the race of her heart seemed to stop in its tracks. Then he was spinning on again, and the dance slowed and stopped, leaving Lina breathless and dizzy in its wake.

The men gathered around, slapping each on the back and laughing as they caught their breath. Lina realized she was still leaning forward with her lips parted. She sat up abruptly, feeling her cheeks grow warm.

"Are you well, child?" Wichapi's voice spoke beside her.

Lina looked down at her. The older woman cradled little Winona in her arms, her shrewd dark eyes staring straight into Lina's soul. She managed a smile. "Yes, thank you, Wichapi. I'm fine."

"Good." Wichapi reached up, touching Lina's cheek. "I'm glad your head has healed so nicely over the past two weeks."

"It has. Your medicines are wonderful," said Lina.

"We've been using those medicines for hundreds of years." Wichapi chuckled softly. "They're even older than I am." Her face grew sad, and she looked down at Winona, running her fingertips over the child's smooth cheeks. "I only wish they could have saved this little one's mother."

"Hotah never talks about his wife," said Lina.

"He still grieves her. It's been a year, yet sometimes I feel like

Mina's spirit is haunting him." Wichapi sighed. "She died giving birth to little Winona, and it shattered him. He loved her more than he loved his own soul."

"I'm sure he did," said Lina softly.

"Winona is so much like her," said Wichapi. "Beautiful, kind – and clever, too."

"She is." Lina laughed. "I'm amazed at how quickly she's learned the games I've been teaching her."

"Just like Mina." Wichapi sighed.

Lina laid a hand on the older woman's shoulder, trying to think of a way to make her feel better somehow. "Thank you so much for taking me in," she said. "You've all been so kind to me. Everyone back East thinks all sorts of silly things about you, but you've been lovely."

"And so have you," Wichapi returned with a smile. "Especially to Winona. She loves you, you know."

Lina heard the distant rumble of Hotah's voice. She looked up. He was still some way away from them, speaking with the men, and she couldn't make out the words. Still, the sound of his voice made something tremble deep inside her.

"No wonder Hotah is always so quiet," she said.

"He didn't talk much even before Mina died. You'd be surprised at how much quieter he used to be before you came," said Wichapi.

"Truly?" Lina stared at her, a strange longing leaping in her heart.

"Yes." Wichapi laid a hand on her arm. "We will all miss you when you go back to Planter's Point."

*Planter's Point.* Lina let out a small sigh, thinking of this Corbin Wedge that she'd come out here to marry. Could he equal the intensity in Hotah's eyes? Her cheeks flushed again, and she pushed the thought aside. She had to go, she knew. Corbin had paid her way out here, after all; it was only right for her to go to him. Yet the stars were so bright here, and the people so friendly. She leaned back a little. She would go to Planter's Point, but her head still hurt sometimes in the evenings. She'd go, but not yet. Not yet.

"I'll miss you, too," she whispered. She was looking at Hotah as she spoke.

The sound of Lina's laughter rolled over Hotah's shoulders as gently as raindrops. He realized that he was smiling, too, as she struggled to stop laughing so that she could finish telling her story. The words came out in little gasps through her mirth.

"Straight into – the – bathtub," she gasped, giggling uncontrollably. "Should have – seen his – face." She dissolved into peals of laughter, and Hotah couldn't help a low chuckle alongside her. Her story, which was difficult to make out through the giggles but seemed to involve her younger brother, a cat, and a tin bath, was funny; but it was her face that delighted him. It was filled with such clear and childlike joy. She reminded him of Winona.

She reminded him of Mina.

A familiar pang of agony shot through him, yet it was muffled somehow by something else: something that grew in him when she finally stopped laughing and looked up at him. "Did you have any brothers and sisters?" she asked.

"A sister," said Hotah. "She married into a neighboring tribe to strengthen our alliance."

Lina sighed, leaning back against the log and extending her thin white feet toward the smoldering coals of the campfire. They must have been sitting out here for hours, Hotah realized. No one else was awake except for a cricket that serenaded them from somewhere in the deep grass surrounding the village. "Marrying a stranger for the good of her family," she said softly. "I know how that feels."

"She was willing," said Hotah.

"I'm sure she was. If she was anything like you, she'd do anything to protect her people," said Lina, looking up at him.

He was momentarily dumbstruck by her eyes; they were the brightest he'd ever seen, the color of shoots in the spring. "Actually, she reminded me of you," he murmured.

A smile flickered over her lips. "I would never have left my family unless they needed me to," she said. Her smile faltered, and she looked away. "I don't want to leave your family either."

*I want you to stay.* Hotah bit back the words. What was he thinking? He'd never felt this way about a woman other than Mina, and this woman was already betrothed. She belonged to another man, and yet the smooth lines of her neck begged to be kissed as she stared down at the dirt. She looked so much simpler, yet so much more beautiful, than when she'd arrived in her tattered yellow dress.

Wearing one of Wichapi's buckskin suits, with a cloak that Wichapi had made just for her and edged with a flowing fringe of leather strips, she looked less like some girl from the city and more like she belonged here. He could only barely hold back his desire, reaching out instead to touch her shoulder with his fingertips. She looked up, her eyes vulnerable. There was so much that he wanted to say, but he couldn't say it. He just wanted her to keep talking.

"You must miss them very much," he said.

"Oh, I do. I've never been away from them for more than a day, let alone three weeks." Lina blinked, and Hotah saw a tear shimmering in the corner of her eye. She looked down again, her hands knotted in her lap. "They must be so afraid for me. I hope they didn't hear about the train robbery, or they'd think the worst..." She sucked in a breath. "I know I have to go back to Planter's Point once my head is better again, for their sake. I-I hope to be able to send money home to them once I'm wed. I would do anything for them."

She'd sounded at first like she was trying to convince herself, but the last sentence roared with a strength that Hotah had seldom seen before. "Have I ever told you about wolves?" he said.

She glanced sideways at him, her eyes dancing with curiosity. "Wolves?"

"Yes." Hotah reached up, unable to stop himself, and hooked a strand of her shining hair back behind her ear. She shuddered a little at his touch but didn't pull away. "A wolf pack consists of a mother and father, as well as their adult cubs," he said. "One time, a group of us had gone out to hunt a herd of elk. We were tracking them through the woods, knowing a wolf pack was moving through the area at the same time, when we came upon the den. It was filled with little cubs, and their mother was nowhere in sight. One of the younger men wanted to take a cub for himself, and I was trying to stop him when I heard something growling."

"Was it the cubs' mother?" Lina whispered, hanging on his every word.

Hotah shook his head. "No. She was out hunting – I'd seen her with the cubs before, and she had black fur. When we turned around, the wolf coming toward us was a young she-wolf, white as snow." He smiled. "She was the sister of the cubs, and she was ready to fight to the death for them."

"What did you do?" asked Lina.

"We got away. It doesn't matter, though. What I'm trying to say is that I never saw anyone so fierce to defend children that were not her own, until now." Hotah leaned a little closer. His fingers moved along the dirt until they found Lina's; they were soft as feathers in his gentle grip. She did not pull her hand away. Her lips were slightly parted, palest pink as her eyes filled his. "You are a she-wolf, Lina," he whispered.

She wasn't moving. She wasn't breathing, but her eyes filled him with something that burned. He leaned closer, and when she didn't move away or tremble, he kissed her. She hesitated for an instant, her lips freezing on his own; then her hand came up, and tentatively encircled his neck. Sparks flew over Hotah's skin. He followed her hand up the smooth length of her arm to her face and cupped it in both of his hands, losing himself in her, allowing himself to be borne away on the sheer glorious tide of her.

He only stopped kissing her when his air ran out. When she sat back, her eyes were shining as she stared at him.

"Hotah," she whispered, her fingertips trembling on his cheek. She smiled, and it struck straight into his soul. He'd made her happy, but only for a moment. Soon she would be torn away from him.

And he'd just made it worse.

He rose, taking her hand in both of his own. He didn't know what to say. He could only pray his eyes would do the talking. "Good night, Lina," he said softly and dropped her hand.

It took all of his strength not to look back as he walked away.

Lina did not sleep that night. She lay wrapped in buffalo skins on a bed of grass, staring up at the paintings that chased each other over the interior of the tipi, and relived the moment over and over when Hotah's lips had met her own. His hair had fallen around her like a curtain, smelling like warm embers and musk, and she had felt something rise in her that she'd never felt before. Something that had taken her breath away.

"What are you doing, Lina?" she whispered.

She knew the answer. As impossible as it was, as unlikely as it was, and as unfulfilled as it would remain – she was falling in love.

Hotah's horse ran from him the moment he set foot in the wooden enclosure. The animal moved with the rippling grace of a river, rushing across the enclosure in a few powerful strides, its muscles breaking like waves beneath its skin. When it reached the far end of the enclosure, it wheeled around and stood looking at him, its eyes glittering with distrust.

"Peta!" Hotah let out the name in a burst of anger. "What are you doing, boy?"

Peta watched him warily as he approached, holding out a hand. "Come here, you stupid horse," Hotah growled under his breath. "We need to go." He lunged, grabbing at the stallion's mane, but Peta slipped aside like a flame and galloped off again. Frustration bubbled over in Hotah's heart, and he flung down the bridle in a temper. "I'll go on foot, then!" he yelled. Peta just snorted at him, shaking his mane.

"Hotah!"

It was Mama. She was standing by the rails, watching him with a mixture of worry and disapproval. "What are you doing?" she called.

Hotah sighed. The sight of her simmered his frustration away, leaving only an aching confusion. He scooped up the bridle and came toward her.

"Being a fool," he said. "I know Peta won't come to me when I'm like this."

Mama folded her arms. "I think you're being a fool in more

ways than one, *ciksi*, if you're doing what I think you're doing."

"What do you mean?" said Hotah.

"Where are you going?"

Hotah looked away. He'd known Mama would try to stop him; that was why he was trying to sneak away from the village this early in the morning.

"Hunting," he said. "We need meat."

"That's nonsense, and you know it," said Mama. "Mato brought back an entire elk bull just three days ago." She paused. "Hotah, you can't run from her."

"I have to," said Hotah tiredly. "What else can I do?"

"Speak to her. Tell her how you feel," said Mama.

"She's marrying a man in Planter's Point."

"She hasn't married him yet. No one can force her to do it if she's fallen in love with you."

Hotah closed his eyes, thinking of the way she'd kissed him. There was no use denying it. "She has to do it, Mama," he said. "The man has a lot of money. She needs it for her family."

"We can do something…" Mama began.

"No." Hotah shook his head. "No, we can't."

She was watching him piercingly, the way she used to when he was a boy trying to hide his escapades from her, and she saw through him now just as she had back then. "Is this about money, or about your heart?" she asked softly. "Mina would have liked her, Hotah. She wouldn't expect you to be alone for the rest of your life."

The mention of his wife's name branded a blazing scar across Hotah's heart. He stepped back, his hands trembling on the bridle. "I'll see you in a few days, Mama."

"She might not be here when you get back," said Mama.

Hotah was already walking away. This time, Peta allowed himself to be bridled. "Then let her go," Hotah said roughly.

"Hotah!"

He didn't listen. He couldn't. He threw himself onto the bare back of his horse and turned his head to the open gate, his hands shaking on the reins. "Go," he growled. "Go!"

Peta fled out into the sunrise, leaving the village behind in moments. Leaving it all behind.

# CHAPTER 9

Lina stepped out of her tipi into a sweet summer morning, feeling refreshed by her quick bath in the stream. She ran her fingers nervously over her braided hair. Wichapi had shown her how to make two neat braids like she wore herself; she hoped Hotah would like it. Despite the lack of sleep that tugged at the back of her eyes, she felt excitement fluttering in the pit of her stomach.

Wichapi was crouched by the fire, stirring a pot of beans. Lina all but skipped over to her. "Good morning, Wichapi."

The older woman turned, scrambling to smile. "Hello, Lina," she said. "Did you sleep well?"

"No, but it's all right," said Lina, grinning. "Have you seen Hotah this morning?"

Wichapi hesitated, and something guarded rose in her eyes that made Lina's heart tremble. "Yes," she said slowly.

"Well, where is he?" Lina felt her smile fading. "I'd like to talk to him."

Wichapi put down her spoon and turned to Lina. "He's not here," she said softly.

Lina stepped back, shock breaking over her like a cold ocean wave, leaving her soaked and breathless. "He's not? Where is he?"

"He's just gone out hunting," said Wichapi, her tone soothing. "He'll be back in a couple of days."

"Hunting?" Lina shook her head. "But Mato brought that elk just a few days ago. Why would Hotah go hunting?"

Wichapi must have heard the desperation in her voice. "It's all right, Lina," she said. "He'll be back. I promise. He just needs to be with the spirits..." She paused, studying Lina with quiet eyes. "You must understand that this is not easy for him."

Lina sat down abruptly on one of the logs, feeling tears building like a storm in her chest. She tried to swallow them back. She should have known all along that he would regret that kiss, that it was nothing more than a moment of foolish passion. Doubt touched her; there was something so genuine about the way his hands had moved on her, something that went far beyond mere desire, something deep and powerful that tugged at her. But clearly, whatever it had been, Hotah had thought better of it now.

"He regrets it," she whispered, a hot tear running down her cheek.

"No, no." Wichapi sat down beside her, wrapping an arm around her shoulders. "Don't think that."

"He does." Lina dashed away the tear, sniffing angrily. "But maybe he's right. In fact…" She took a deep breath, trying to calm herself. "I know he's right. I'm betrothed to another man, even if I've never met him." She swallowed hard. "I should never have stayed this long."

Wichapi was watching her with sorrowful eyes. Lina swallowed against her pain. "He did the right thing by leaving," she said. "It's brought me to my senses."

"Lina," said Wichapi, gently.

"Please," Lina whispered. "Please don't try to talk me out of this, Wichapi. I love you so much, and Winona, and I've loved staying with the Lakota, and I love…" She paused, closing her eyes, feeling the tears escape. She couldn't finish the sentence. "But I have to go now, for my own family's sake."

Wichapi gave her a kind squeeze. "I won't argue with you, then, much as I would like to," she said softly. "But I do have one request to make."

"I owe you that much," Lina sniffled. "You've been so good to me, scooping me up and looking after me even though I was a perfect stranger to you."

Wichapi's eyes were soft. "Wait until Hotah gets back," she said.

Lina drew back. She didn't know if she'd be able to look into those dark eyes again. "Wichapi…"

"Listen to me." Wichapi's tone had a gentle firmness that pressed Lina into silence. "I know you're disappointed that he's gone, Lina, but I know my son. He's gone hunting to clear his head, and once it's cleared, you might want to hear what he has to say."

Lina shook her head. "I can't," she said. "I have to go. I have to marry Corbin Wedge… no matter what I believe. For my family's sake." She brushed away her tears with the back of her sleeve.

"Then wait for him so that he can take you to Planter's Point," said Wichapi. "You can't undertake that journey alone in this harsh country, Lina. We're short a man now that Hotah has gone away. Just wait for his return and let him ride to the town with you."

Lina closed her eyes, allowing herself to picture it just for a moment: a day's ride over these wild plains, Hotah at her side, just the two of them. Her heart raced even though she knew that it would be their last day together. She looked over at Wichapi, trying to hold back the longing that ached in her heart.

"All right," she said. "I'll wait until Hotah gets back. That will also give me a chance to figure out how I'm going to say goodbye to Winona." The thought made her throat tighten. "I'm going to miss her."

"She'll miss you, too. We all will," said Wichapi.

Lina closed her eyes again as the older woman drew her into a kind embrace. This time, she allowed the tears to flow freely down her cheeks. She couldn't believe how quickly the Lakota tribe had become her family.

And she couldn't believe that she was about to say goodbye to her family for the second time.

The breeze stirred Hotah's hair, running its cool fingertips over his face where he sat in the long grass. Hunger gnawed at his stomach, but it was nothing compared to the ache in his heart, which had only intensified since he'd come to the top of this hill yesterday morning. He'd told Wichapi he'd gone hunting; he hadn't told her that he was hunting for something more than meat.

He was hunting for reason.

Opening his eyes, Hotah stared dully at the little mound of

earth in front of him. A year ago, it had been a fresh brown scar among the green grass, throbbing in the landscape like the wound in his heart. Now, it was completely covered over with grass. When he looked closely, he could see a clutch of wildflowers blooming among the green vegetation, somewhere near the top of the mound.

"Mina." Hotah's lips were dry. He sipped from the waterskin lying beside him, then tried again. "Mina, what am I going to do?"

He wished that some kind of a sign would fall from the wide blue sky; an eagle swooping down to land upon Mina's grave, perhaps, or the answer to his heart's great question spelled out in white puffs of cloud. Better yet, he wished that she could be here beside him right now. Even now, it was so easy to imagine her: the lustrous dark eyes, the twin braids down her back, the softness of her skin against his own. The thought brought a deep pang to his heart. He had never felt for a woman the way he'd felt for Mina… not until now.

He reached out and pressed the palm of his hand against the mound of the grave. "I'm frightened, Mina," he whispered. "I'm frightened of leaving you behind."

The breeze stirred his hair again, and a memory came back to him: a day that had come earlier that summer, when he'd been standing at this same spot and heard Winona's sweet voice calling to him. Mama had come to him then, calling him back home to the tribe. The most poignant part of the memory was the way Mama had referred to Mina's death. She hadn't called it dying or passing away.

*Mina walked on.* Hotah raised his eyes to the horizon, feeling tears on his cheeks. Mina was gone, but not forever, and not from all existence. She wasn't gone like water into sand; she was gone like a hunting party, like a river draining into the sea. She had gone somewhere else. She had gone on before him.

"I wouldn't be leaving you behind," Hotah whispered. "You already left me behind. And where you've gone, you don't need me anymore."

The ring of truth in the words seemed to lift something from his chest, relieving him, like the bridle being removed from a horse. Mina was safe now, safer than he could ever have kept her. But Lina… she was right here.

"I've been a fool." Hotah scrambled to his feet. He glanced over his shoulder to where Peta was picketed and grazing nearby. "I have to get back."

He turned away, pausing at the last moment to blow a kiss back over his shoulder. He could almost feel it settling like a feather on Mina's grave.

"I love you forever," he whispered.

The doors of his heart felt thrown wide open. He ran to his horse, free at last.

It was only a few minutes' brisk canter from Mina's grave to the village. Peta was hardly winded when Hotah spotted the twist of black smoke rising from the trees surrounding the village, and his heart thumped hard with excitement. He would tell Lina everything the moment he set eyes on her. He would tell her that she made his heart turn cartwheels, that her eyes held the key to his heart, that he had said farewell to Mina – and that his heart was wide open now to her.

It took all of his willpower to slow Peta to a walk for the last few hundred feet to allow the horse's body a chance to cool off. He wanted to gallop into that village, sweep Lina from her feet, and kiss her the way he'd kissed her two nights ago – only this time, there would be nothing holding him back.

But when Hotah reached the village and sprang down from his horse, looking around eagerly for Lina, he realized that he would be doing no such thing. There was a small bundle sitting on one of the logs around the fireplace: it seemed to be wrapped with buckskin but secured with a thin strip of yellow satin. Leaving his horse at the edge of the clearing, Hotah walked up to it and reached out to touch the satin. The buckskin wrapping turned out to be familiar. It was the cloak that Wichapi had made for Lina.

Buffalo hide rustled. Hotah looked up as Lina stepped out of his tipi, tying the strings of her bonnet. He hadn't seen her wear it since the day he'd found her; blood had left a faint pink stain on one side of it. She was wearing her yellow dress again.

"Hotah." Lina hesitated. "You're back."

There was something reserved about her that hadn't been there last time he saw her. It certainly hadn't been present in her kiss. His arms longed to be thrown around her, but instead, Hotah straightened and stepped back.

"You're leaving?" he said.

Lina nodded, her eyes guarded as she watched him. "I have to. I have to marry Corbin Wedge so that I can send money back to my family." She faltered, dropping her gaze to the ground. "It's the only way," she whispered.

*Stay.* Hotah wanted to scream the word to her, to sing it. To breathe it into her ear so that his breath would touch her skin. But he couldn't. She was right. His currency was meat and leather; he couldn't provide for a family that needed money.

"I was just waiting for you," Lina said. "Your mother said that you would ride to Planter's Point with me."

She raised her eyes to his own, and he saw himself reflected in her: the same longing that burned in his chest blazed in her eyes.

The world had never felt more cruel. For a moment, Hotah

considered flinging himself onto his horse and riding out onto those plains, and never looking back. But her jade eyes called him. He couldn't give up a day riding with her, even if it was only one day.

"All right," he said softly. "We leave in the morning."

She reached out, touching her fingertips to his palm in a way that made goosebumps rise on his skin.

"Thank you," she said.

Hotah could not reply.

# CHAPTER 10

There was silence the next morning as they set out over the plains, yet it was not for lack of something to say. In fact, Lina felt that there was so much she wanted to say that it was smothering her. It lay over her shoulders, wet and dark and heavy as a thundercloud, squeezing the words inside her into silence.

She hadn't ridden much before, and certainly not bareback, but when Hotah reassured her that she'd be safe, she couldn't find it in her heart to be afraid. She sat still, her fingers tangled in the coarse mane of the waddling pony that Wichapi had lent her. It matched Hotah's flashy red-coated horse stride for stride as they left the trees behind and walked out onto the plains. Hotah's eyes were fixed straight ahead. Lina could not bring herself to stop staring at him. He was so straight and proud and perfect as he rode that even the splendor of a golden sunrise over the expanse of plains couldn't distract Lina's attention from him.

It was so strange to think that, in just a few weeks' time, she would be married – and not to Hotah. She didn't even know what this Corbin Wedge looked like or how he would treat her. But she knew Hotah in his every mood; she knew his joy and sorrow, his anger and patience. She knew the feel of his hands. She knew the touch of his lips on her own. She knew the way he laughed as he played with little Winona and the thoughtless compassion that had led him to bring her to the village, and she wanted to know so much more, but she never would because tonight she would sleep in the home of a man she'd never laid eyes on before. She'd marry soon.

She wished she could be married to Hotah.

It was late in the morning that they reached the train tracks where Hotah had found her. His horse shook its mane and snorted at the flash of the iron tracks in the sun; it was the first unnatural thing Lina had laid eyes on in weeks, and to her eyes it looked ugly, hateful. Blackmore, the thug who'd thrown her from the train, flashed through her memory. She shuddered.

Hotah reined in his horse and looked over at her. "Are you all right?" His voice was deep, surging through her like electricity.

"Just… remembering what happened here." Lina shivered. "I would be dead if it weren't for you."

"I couldn't have left you," said Hotah.

Lina gazed up into his eyes. He couldn't leave her then. Could she leave him now? For a wild moment, she wanted to seize his hand, to beg him to pull her onto his horse behind him, wheel around and ride back to the tribe as fast as the animal could run. She wanted to scoop Winona back into her arms again and still the torrent of tears that the baby had cried when Lina had said goodbye. She wanted to grip Wichapi's hand and think of her as a mother. She wanted to kiss him again…

Hotah seemed to read her thoughts, and his eyes intensified as he leaned a little closer to her. Lina closed her eyes, trying to calm her thundering heart. *No.* She couldn't go back. She could never go back again; for the sake of Joe and Maggie, Peter and Amy, Mama and Papa… she had to go on. She had never loved anything more than she loved them, and the fact that Hotah now equaled it couldn't stop her from doing what she had to do to protect them.

"Are we following the tracks to the town?" she asked, sitting back so abruptly on her plump little horse that it let out a grunt of surprise.

Hotah's eyes clouded with disappointment, but he kept it out of his voice. "Yes," he said. "We'll be there by late afternoon."

He turned and urged his horse to walk briskly into the western horizon. Lina's horse followed, and she held on to its mane, praying that the day would somehow end well.

"Here we are," said Hotah. For the first time since leaving the village, Lina could detect a note of bitterness in his voice. "Planter's Point."

Lina could hardly believe that the cluster of buildings at the foot of the hill could qualify as a town at all. There were fewer buildings here than in a single city block in Boston: a row of small houses squared off over the single street with what appeared to be businesses. Judging by the laughter coming from one, which drifted up on an evening breeze to where Hotah and Lina sat on their horses on the hilltop, it had to be a saloon.

The grass had been pushed back from the buildings; the earth was bare, the street unpaved, the boardwalks almost as dusty as the road itself. The country had grown more and more hilly as Lina and Hotah headed further west, and the town itself was surrounded with steep hills strewn with boulders. Lina could see a small and desperate copse of ash trees clinging to the side of a hill on the far side of town, a dark splash in the bleak and colorless landscape.

"This is my new home," said Lina softly.

"I suppose it is," said Hotah. He looked over at her, concern in his face, and seemed for a moment as though he wanted to say something. Instead, he looked away and kicked his horse forward.

Lina's body ached as her horse followed him down into the town. The closer she got, the more she could make out, and the more her misgivings about this place grew. The first building they reached was utterly empty, its broken windows staring at her like soulless eyes, tumbleweeds piled up on the inside. Other houses seemed to have people in them, but some of their windows were boarded up, and there was no laughter from inside.

But what struck Lina the most was the expressions of the people she saw walking on the boardwalk or sitting on their narrow porches. Their eyes watched her, first with horror, then – as they turned to Hotah – with a kind of bitter hatred that tasted black and thick on the back of Lina's tongue. Hotah shifted uncomfortably on his horse, but he kept his eyes ahead.

"Where does this Mr. Wedge live?" he asked tightly.

"I don't know," said Lina. "I… I lost his letter. It was in my bag when they robbed the train." She swallowed. "Maybe we should ask for directions."

Hotah glanced at her, then at the nearest person: an old woman working the handle of the pump in the middle of the town's tiny square. She'd frozen with her hand on the pump, and her eyes bored into them, hard and cold.

"Maybe," he said reluctantly.

"Let's try the jailhouse," Lina suggested. "Maybe the sheriff will be there."

"Sheriff Miller?" Hotah's shoulders relaxed a little. "Yes. He's a good sort. We were friends as children – he'll be sure to help us."

They turned toward the jailhouse, tucked away in the far corner of town, and ran the gauntlet of icy stares up to the front porch. Hotah dismounted and tapped on the door. "Sheriff Miller?" he called.

Lina decided it was wisest not to get off her horse; her body ached, and she feared her legs might crumple underneath her. She sat and waited as loud footsteps echoed through the little building. When the door opened, a portly, mustachioed man looked up at Hotah in surprise. His mustache bristled like a scrubbing brush.

"Hotah!" he said. "As I live and breathe. I haven't seen you in – well, it must be a year now." He laid a hand on Hotah's arm. "I was so sad to hear about Mina."

Hotah forced a smile. "Thank you for your compassion, Jake."

"Of course. Come on in," said Sheriff Miller. He peered around Hotah at Lina, and his eyebrows rose. "And your lady friend is welcome to a bite of supper, too."

"We don't have time for that. I'm sorry," said Hotah. "This

young woman came out West seeking her husband – she is a Mail Order Bride. She was hurt in a robbery and my mother cared for her. Now that she's well again, I've brought her to meet her husband, but she lost his address during the robbery."

Sheriff Miller's eyes grew dark. "These train robbers have ruined many lives in this town," he said. "You've seen for yourself that it's not the same place as it was when you were last here."

"I did see it has changed," said Hotah. "And so has the way that people look at me."

"They're scared. They've been robbed so badly," said Sheriff Miller. He sighed. "I'm sorry, Hotah."

"It's all right. Please, we just need those directions." Hotah turned to Lina. "What did you say your fiancé's name was?" He squeezed the word *fiancé* out like it tasted bad.

"Wedge," said Lina. "Corbin Wedge."

Sheriff Miller's shoulders stiffened in a way that made fear ripple through Lina's heart. She stared at him. "Is something wrong, sheriff?"

Sheriff Miller cleared his throat. "N-no," he said. "Not at all." He forced a smile, but his eyes were wary. "Corbin's cabin isn't far – just up that hill there." He pointed to the hill with the grove of trees that Lina had noticed earlier. "Head up the trail through those trees and you'll be right on top of it."

Hotah was studying Sheriff Miller with a strange expression. Eventually, he said, "All right. Thank you, Jake."

"Anytime." Sheriff Miller's eyes softened. "Don't be a stranger, Hotah. Our people need to remember that we're friends with the Lakota."

Hotah gave one curt nod and turned to swing back onto his horse. "Come on, Lina," he said. "We're nearly there."

Lina glanced back once as they rode out of the town. The sheriff was still standing on his porch, staring after them, and his right hand was resting on the six-shooter at his hip.

Jake had been right. Corbin Wedge's cabin was easy to find, if only because whoever had built it had chosen to situate it in an area where no one else would want to live. Peta was blowing hard, exhausted by the steep and rocky trail, when they emerged from the trees and into a clearing that dropped away steeply on one side into the river; the other side ended in a craggy cliff that rose up sharply toward the darkening sky. Hotah could only imagine that whoever built the cabin had brought it up, plank by plank, on the back of some poor tired pack mule.

It crouched, now, on the far end of the clearing, right by the cliff down into the river; a miserable, drafty thing with a thin chimney that coughed a sad little trickle of smoke into the air.

Hotah glanced back. Lina was white-faced and tight-lipped where she sat astride Mama's pony behind him. Her face was smeared with dust from the travel, but he thought he might spot a glimmer of tears on it in the fading light.

"This is it," she said, trying bravely to smile.

Hotah swallowed. He only had one last chance with her, a last few moments to hear her voice. "Are you sure you want to do this?" he said softly.

Lina stared at him. For a glorious moment, he thought she might tell him no, she wasn't sure – in fact, she wanted to come back home with him. Instead, her shoulders squared. "Yes," she said. "For my family."

Hotah had never loved her more than in that moment. "All right," he said softly, springing down from his horse. He helped her down; the pressure of her fingers on his palm made him tremble, and he let go as soon as she was steady on her feet.

Hotah didn't like the feeling that crawled over his skin as he walked toward the cabin. Lina was close behind him, and he tried to resist the urge to shield her with his body as he reached the front door. Raising his knuckles, he went to knock, but before they could meet the wood the door banged open and the twin barrels of a shotgun was aimed right between his eyes.

"Git away, you filthy savage!" roared a coarse voice from the shadows of the cabin. "Leave the lady and begone with you!"

Hotah contained his anger with difficulty. He put a hand on the barrel and pushed it down to the ground with a slow, smooth movement. "Are you Corbin Wedge?" he said.

A white, pinched face sneered at him from inside the shadows. "I am," he growled, "and I'm afraid of no one."

"Neither am I," said Hotah calmly. "I've brought you your bride."

Corbin's eyes widened. He lowered the gun, and Hotah stepped aside so that Lina could move forward. Corbin looked as though someone had hit him between the eyes with a sledgehammer. His stubbly jaw slackened, his eyes popping as he looked her up and down in a smooth movement that made Hotah's fingers curl into a fist.

"Well, aren't you the finest-looking creature that I've ever clapped eyes on." Corbin gasped. "Are you Lina Sterling?"

Lina was trembling slightly. "Yes, sir," she said. "That's me."

"Well!" Corbin let out a crow of delight, stowing the shotgun behind the door and walking out to Lina. He laid a grubby hand on each of her shoulders and looked her up and down, his face appreciative. "You splendid thing, you." He gave her a gap-toothed grin. "I thought you'd never come."

"I was hurt on my way here," said Lina. "Hotah's family took care of me until I was well enough to travel." She shot Hotah a look. He expected her to look scared; instead, her eyes were imploring, determined. He realized, with a horrible jolt, that Lina didn't want him to rescue her from this situation. "I'm sorry it's taken me so long," she added.

"Never mind, dear, never mind," leered Corbin. He gave Hotah a quick look that made his skin crawl. Hotah had never hated anyone before, but he realized in that moment that he hated Corbin with a dark and burning passion.

"Come on," said Corbin. "I'm sure you're dying for some good company and real food." He put an expansive arm around Lina's shoulders. "Come inside and warm yourself by the fire. I have some real bacon just ready to put into the pan."

"Sounds nice," Lina managed. She didn't look at Hotah, but he could hear that she was holding back tears.

"Don't worry your pretty head now, honey." Corbin led her into his cabin. "You're safe with me."

He slammed the door behind him, leaving Hotah outside, staring at the closed door, his hands clenched by his sides, the hair standing straight up on the back of his neck. It took him a few moments to uproot himself from where he stood and walk back to where the horses waited at the edge of the trees. He didn't like this – any of this. He didn't like Corbin, he didn't like this shady little cabin in the middle of nowhere, and he especially didn't like Jake's reaction when Lina had told him the name of her fiancé.

Lina had told him that this Corbin Wedge was a successful businessman, but Hotah wondered what kind of businessman would live in a secluded cabin in a desolate place like this. He feared that nothing Lina hoped for, not even money for her family, would come of this situation.

He'd planned to camp in the plains just beyond Planter's Point tonight, but now he knew there was no chance of that happening. Collecting the horses, he rode carefully in the growing dusk, leaving the copse of trees behind to reach the top of the cliff that overlooked the cabin. There, he built no fire. He just picketed the horses near some good grazing and crawled to the edge of the cliff on his belly, keeping his tomahawk and bow close at hand.

The night was absolutely still. A generous full moon scattered abundant silver light into the clearing; the yellow firelight in the windows of the cabin was feeble by comparison. Hotah listened, but all he could hear from below was quiet conversation, the sizzle of something frying.

It was almost an hour later that he heard the hoofbeats. Looking up over the copse of trees and the silver line of the trail they'd followed to the cabin, he saw them: approaching horsemen. From this distance, it was hard to tell, but he thought they could be masked.

And he thought they looked familiar.

## CHAPTER 12

The interior of Corbin's cabin was as loose and sloppy as his language. Lina had to keep her head ducked to avoid the miscellany of objects – pots and pans, hams, the grisly trophy of a deer's head, guns, sheathed knives – hanging from the crooked rafters as she made her way nervously from the small stool where she'd been perched by the fire to the low table in one corner of the room. Corbin had just laid out two tin plates on the table; his hands were shaking as he scooped out some beans from a rusty tin, joining the bacon that he'd just finished cooking.

"Th-there you are," he said, giving her a nervous glance. "I hope you don't mind beans."

"Not at all, Mr. Wedge," said Lina, forcing herself to smile.

"Please – Corbin," he said. He sat down opposite her and

stared at her for a moment, seeming tongue-tied.

Lina didn't know what to say. She'd only been in this cabin for an hour, and already, she wanted to scream. *How am I going to stay here for a lifetime?* But she'd seen the moneybags in the other corner of the room. She had to get some of that sent to her family, even if she was dooming herself to a life sentence of heartache.

At least Corbin himself seemed fairly harmless – if boring. She picked up her fork and sampled the beans. They were watery, tasteless. "These are lovely," she managed.

"Oh, I like beans," said Corbin. He shoveled up a great mouthful and spoke through it. "Pity they give me terrible wind."

Lina tried to swallow back the despair that filled her heart. *How am I going to do this?*

She'd just stuffed another mouthful of the nasty beans into her mouth, hoping to avoid having to say something, when there was a great clattering sound from outside. Corbin leaped to his feet, his face growing ashen.

"What's wrong?" Lina asked.

"Nothing." Corbin grabbed his shotgun again from behind the door. "Stay inside."

Lina felt herself trembling. She rose, turning to face the door as Corbin peered through the keyhole. For a wild moment, she wondered if Hotah had come to save her. But it had sounded like numerous horses coming across the clearing toward them.

Corbin let out a word that made Lina's ears burn. He cocked the shotgun, then pushed the door open, and Lina took an eager step forward, ready to see him…

She froze in her tracks.

She was staring directly into the sparkling eyes of Max Blackmore.

Corbin's shotgun was poking into Blackmore's chest, but the robber didn't even look at it. Instead, he was staring at Lina, the moonlight glittering on his messy blond hair, and there was something dangerous in his gaze. Corbin was saying something, and there were other men behind Blackmore, but Lina's entire world had been distilled to her terror as she stared into Blackmore's eyes.

He knew her. She knew he did, and she quaked to the core as she remembered his cruel grip on his arm.

Corbin was twittering something. Lina could barely make out the words through the rush of blood in her ears. "I told you, I never want to see you again!" He poked Blackmore in the chest with the shotgun. "Get away from my cabin!"

Blackmore blinked. The spell broke, and Lina sank into her chair, staring. Blackmore looked down at Corbin and his face relaxed into a gold-toothed grin.

"Oh, Corbin, Corbin!" he boomed, flicking the shotgun aside with one finger. He squeezed his giant frame through the doorway. "We all know you won't stay away for long."

"I'm going to stay away," Corbin said. His weaselly face was mixed with fear and determination as he clutched the shotgun. "I told you, Max, I'm done with crime. I had a lot of time to think after that good-for-nothin' sheriff shot me in the chest, and I figured with my cut of the train robbery back in February, I've got what I need to live a quiet life now."

"Quiet life?" Blackmore let out a chuckle and sank onto the stool by the fire. The other men stayed outside; the stool creaked under his weight. "Corbin Wedge, living a quiet life? You've been a robber all your life, boy. What are you going to do now?"

Corbin shot Lina a frightened glance. "I'm going to stay here in my cabin," he said sharply.

"No, you ain't. The boss wants you back," said Blackmore. "We need your lock-pickin' skills on our next job."

"Well, you're not going to get them," said Corbin. "I told you, I'm done. I'm staying right here with the gold I've got left. Maybe I'll pan in the river or something – I don't know." He raised his chin a little. "I've even got me a little wife now, see?"

Blackmore turned, studying Lina for a moment again with those frightening eyes.

"I do see," he rumbled.

Lina felt fused to her chair with fear. She couldn't move, and Corbin gave her an uncomfortable look. "Don't you worry, honey," he said. "I'm going to get rid of this oaf right away." He pointed the shotgun at Blackmore again. "Git out of here!"

Blackmore pushed the gun away. "There's something you need to know about your little wife," he sneered.

Corbin hesitated. Blackmore rose and leaned close to him; Lina heard the deep murmur of his voice, but she couldn't make out the words. Corbin's eyes widened. He drew back, staring at Blackmore. "Are you sure?"

Blackmore turned, resting his eyes on Lina. "I never forget the face of a problem," he growled.

Lina backed away against the wall of the cabin, her heart pounding. Corbin was staring at her with disappointment, but there was something cruel and hungry in Blackmore's eyes.

"But she won't tell," Corbin protested. He put down the shotgun and went over to Lina, grabbing her hand; his grip was cold and feeble. "Will you, darlin'? You won't tell anyone that dear old Max was the train robber. Will you?"

"It's a risk we can't take, Corbin," growled Blackmore.

"She'll promise. She'll promise," said Corbin, patting Lina's cheek with a hand that smelled of fear and gunpowder. "She will, won't you, Lina? Go on. Tell him. Say you won't tell a soul. You'll stay here in this cabin as good and quiet as a little mouse, won't you?"

Lina remembered the kick that Blackmore had dealt that young mother back in the train as she protected her child. Something surged inside her, and she locked eyes with the powerful blond man.

"Of course, I'll tell," she said, her voice ringing through the cabin. "You're a robber and a murderer, and you should be in jail."

The hand that slapped deafeningly across her cheek wasn't Blackmore's. It was Corbin's. Lina fell against the wall, gasping, raising a hand to her burning face. Something cold had crept into Corbin's eyes.

"Now look what you done," he barked. "I just wanted a quiet life with a pretty little woman like you, and now you ruined it all. You cost me a fortune!" He shook his head. "So beautiful. Such a waste."

"Your loss," said Blackmore, shrugging. He pulled his revolver from his belt and aimed it between Lina's eyes. "I'll enjoy this," he hissed to her.

Outside, there was a thin sound – the whine of air being cloven in half. It was followed by a meaty slap, and a scream that ended in a gurgle.

"What's that?" Blackmore whipped around.

Corbin's face had turned putty gray. "Oh, it's him," he whimpered. "He's back. He's back."

A gunshot rang out, shaking Lina to her very bones. But then there was another thin hiss, and a howl of pain; the clatter of metal on wood. And then a voice. It was a voice that soared like eagle wings and lifted Lina's heart along with it, rising up among the stars.

"*Hoka hey!*" it cried, echoing from cliff to cliff. "*Hoka hey!*"

Blackmore cursed. "Indians!" he growled. "We'll see about them." He lunged at the door.

"No!" Lina cried, plunging after him as he yanked the door open. She grabbed for his gun, her fingers closing around the cold metal; he whirled, the door crashing open behind him, giving her a glimpse of the starry sky. His fingernails raked over her hands, but she clung to the gun with all of her strength.

Blackmore's face was in her own. He smiled cruelly. "Don't try it, girl," he hissed. "It didn't end well for you last time."

Lina raised her face to his. "You'll soon see about this fighting spirit of mine," she whispered. Then she lunged forward and up, slamming the top of her head into Blackmore's nose and lip. He staggered out of the door, his fingers leaving the gun; Lina raised it at him as he stumbled to a halt, staring at her, blood coursing down his chin.

He laughed, teeth flashing red in the moonlight. "Didn't think that through, did you?" he growled, ripping a second revolver out of his belt.

Lina had just enough time to feel her blood freeze before that whining sound slit the air again. There was a thump, and Blackmore staggered back a step, surprise filling his face. He looked down. The head of an arrow protruded from his chest, blood already seeping into his shirt.

The tall robber fell backward without a sound, and there *he* was, stepping over Blackmore's body, proud and perfect in the moonlight that traced silver fingers across his black hair, his intense eyes bright as twin stars as he walked toward her. Lina lowered the gun, feeling her heart leap.

"Hotah!" she cried.

Her joy was premature. There was a strangled cry from behind her, and a skinny arm was thrown around her neck. Gasping for air, Lina flailed at it with one hand. Strong fingers wrenched the gun out of her hand, and she felt the smooth cold circle of the barrel pressed into the side of her head. She froze.

"Don't move." Corbin's smelly breath hissed on Lina's cheek, but he was addressing Hotah. "Don't move, or I'll blow her brains out."

Tears of terror filled Lina's eyes. "Hotah," she gasped.

"Be still," said Hotah softly.

She stared into his eyes. Corbin gave a breathless laugh in her ear; she could feel his heart hammering against her back. "Now put down that bow," he said. "Real slow."

Hotah lowered his bow. Lina heard the creak as it slackened, and he bent slowly, laying the bow on the ground. The tip of the arrowhead rested on the dirt, but Hotah didn't quite let it go. He met Lina's eyes, and a smile tugged at the corner of his lip.

"*Tecihila*," he said.

"What?" snapped Corbin.

Hotah's hand moved faster than a muzzle flash. Lina barely saw the arrowhead glint in the moonlight before he'd thrown it straight into Corbin's calf, where it crunched into something that sounded like bone. The robber let out a scream in Lina's ear, but the barrel disappeared from her head. She wrenched herself free of his arms and bolted straight for Hotah, not looking back. His bow was already in his hand; she rushed behind him, grabbing his warm, firm arm, and spun to face Corbin. He'd collapsed to the ground, clutching his bleeding calf.

"Don't hurt me," he panted. "Please, don't hurt me."

"Oh, you won't be hurt, son," a slow voice spoke from behind them. "But you'll certainly be hanged."

Hotah and Lina both turned. It was the sheriff. He strode out into the clearing, the silver star of his sheriff's badge gleaming in the moonlight.

"Sheriff Miller," Corbin whimpered.

"Imagine my surprise when I heard this here young lady speak your name." Sheriff Miller tipped back his hat. "'Specially since you're supposed to have been dead for these last six months. I guessed you'd be up here in your hideout, though." He touched Lina's shoulder. "I'm sorry I took so long to get to you, dear – a few of Mr. Wedge's cronies back there gave me some trouble once I came out of hiding after hearing his wonderful little confession to Max Blackmore."

"Y-you knew he was a criminal?" Lina said.

"I've been after Corbin Wedge for a long time, suspecting he was affiliated to Blackmore's gang, but I could never be sure – until now." Sheriff Miller squared his shoulders. "Now he'll rot in jail. I'm sorry for using you as bait, but I'm sure it can all be remedied… say, by the bounties for Corbin Wedge, Max Blackmore, and a few of these other dastardly characters."

"Bounties?" said Hotah.

"Oh, yes. They all have a handsome sum upon their heads." Sheriff Miller grinned. "And you two are the ones who caught them. Those bounties are all yours."

Lina's heart was thundering. She turned to Hotah. "My

family!" she cried. She looked over at Sheriff Miller. "They're in Boston. They need help."

"Darling, those bounties will be more than enough to set up a whole family with a cozy home and a nice new little business." Sheriff Miller laughed. "And pay for a wedding, besides."

He winked at them and then walked back to where Corbin lay. Lina turned to stare up at Hotah. "Did you hear that?" she gasped.

"I think what I heard…" Hotah wrapped his arms around her, "… is that there's nothing standing between the two of us anymore."

Lina felt as though her whole body was filled with fireworks. She gazed up into Hotah's eyes. "What was that you said just now," she whispered, "right before you threw the arrow at Corbin?"

Hotah leaned a little closer and whispered the words to her lips.

"*Tecihila*," he said. "It means 'I love you'."

And this time, when he kissed her, there was no holding back.

# CHAPTER 13

The shining white mare had been a gift from Lina's father. It must have cost Papa a fortune to send the animal in a train all the way from Boston; then again, the little bakery he'd built from the bounty money had erupted into a chain of different stores all over the city, and Papa had quite fortune enough to have done it. Lina smiled at the memory as she walked across the grass to where the herd of horses were grazing down by the stream. The mare was much taller than the stocky mustangs that the natives rode, and she stuck out like a sore thumb, towering over the aging chestnut stallion Peta. Lina guessed that she, too, looked very different from her new family. But like the white mare, she was fitting in on a deeper level.

"Hush, now, *cuwitku*," she whispered, squeezing the small

hand of the child who walked beside her. "You don't want to frighten the little one."

The girl looked up at her. She had Hotah's long, black hair and tan skin, but her eyes were startlingly green, like Lina's. "Is it a little girl or a boy?" she whispered.

"A filly," said Lina. She squeezed the girl's hand. "A girl like you."

"Hurry up!" hissed Winona. She moved a few strides ahead of Lina and her younger half-sister, her strides dancing. She glanced over her shoulder, eyes excited, and Lina was struck by how womanly her figure had become. "I can't wait for you to see this."

The mare lifted her head as Lina and her daughters approached. She let out a gentle whinny, and a tiny foal stumbled out from behind her on new, wobbly legs. The foal's coat was red, streaked with white hairs; its nose and eyes were ringed with white.

"Oooh!" squealed Lina's youngest daughter, softly.

"Shhh." Lina laughed quietly. "You don't want to scare her."

"She's so pretty," said the child.

Hotah appeared from where he'd been stroking Peta's neck. He came over to the little girl and took her free hand. "She's beautiful just like you," he said.

"*Atè!*" The child laughed.

Hotah swept the little girl into his arms, and Lina smiled up at him. The years had only served to make the lines of his face stronger, more beautiful. He kissed the child's forehead. "Hello, my little Mina."

Mina giggled, giving her father a childish kiss on the nose.

"*Mama!*" Winona grabbed Lina's hand. "What are we going to name her?"

"Who?" said Lina.

"The little foal, of course," said Winona impatiently. "You said I could have her, didn't you?"

"Of course, I did." Lina laughed and wrapped an arm around Winona's shoulders. "What do you think?"

"Oh, I don't know. You always give the best names."

Lina knelt down and extended a hand to the foal. It took a step forward, then moved its inexpressibly soft lips across her hand. Her eyes stung with tears of joy. She was so surrounded by love.

"We'll call her *Tecihila*," she said.


The End

CONTINUE READING...

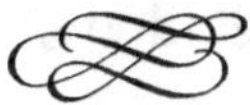

Thank you for reading **Rescuing the Bride! Are you wondering what to read next?** Why not read *The Doctor's Widow??* **Here's a peek for you:**

It was another beautiful spring day at Three Cedars Ranch. Valerie Tait found herself wishing she could enjoy it.

It wasn't that she didn't appreciate the sunshine, and the burgeoning warmth of the weather. Her newly planted garden was already beginning to flourish, radishes and carrots poking their bright green sprouts out of the dark ground. Flocks of geese flew overhead, already beginning their northern migration. Yes, everything seemed to be well on its way to a peaceful and prosperous summer.

Everything, that was, except the Tait family itself.

The ranch, too, was looking a little worse for wear, she had to admit. She did her best to care for the house and keep it clean and neat, but she couldn't repair all the things that were going wrong. And there was quite a list.

It was when the barn door came off its hinges as she went to milk the cows that she decided she needed to buckle down and face up to Reese.

It wasn't going to be easy – her cousin Reese was stubborn, to begin with. And every time she tried to speak to him about something serious, whether it was the ranch or the children, he got that faraway look in his eye that said his mind was on something else – and she knew exactly what.

She couldn't quite blame him. They were coming up on the one-year anniversary of Claire's death. Even Valerie thought about it every day; of course, Reese would be occupied with his thoughts as the ominous day crept up on them. Valerie knew that this was not the best time to be stern with her cousin, but it seemed that there was no way to avoid it, if she wanted to help whip him into shape again.

Besides – she had some news for him, when she thought he could stand hearing it.

But this was not the time for that. Not yet. One thing at a time. She put her news firmly out of mind and went to check on the children.

They were playing in the yard behind the house, a little

fenced-in area that Valerie had built herself. While Reese was out with his cattle, she took charge of caring for the children. But there was far too much to do in the house and the garden; she couldn't be packing one-year-old twins on her hips everywhere she went. She'd need at least three arms. And so, the makeshift playpen was created, full of toys for the twins to keep themselves occupied. Although, she was pretty sure at this point, they were mostly entertained by each other.

**Visit HERE To Read More!**

http://ticahousepublishing.com/mail-order-brides.html

Susannah has always been intrigued with the Western movement - prairie days, mail-order brides, the gold rush, frontier life! As a writer, she's excited to combine her love of story with her love of all that is Western. Presently, Susannah lives in Wyoming with her hubby and their three amazing children.

www.ticahousepublishing.com
contact@ticahousepublishing.com